AREN'T YOU FORGETTING SOMETHING, FIONA?

To librarians, parents, and teachers:

Aren't You Forgetting Something, Fiona? is a Parents Magazine READ ALOUD Original — one title in a series of colorfully illustrated and fun-to-read stories that young readers will be sure to come back to time and time again.

Now, in this special school and library edition of *Aren't You Forgetting Something, Fiona?*, adults have an even greater opportunity to increase children's responsiveness to reading and learning — and to have fun every step of the way.

When you finish this story, check the special section at the back of the book. There you will find games, projects, things to talk about, and other educational activities designed to make reading enjoyable by giving children and adults a chance to play together, work together, and talk over the story they have just read.

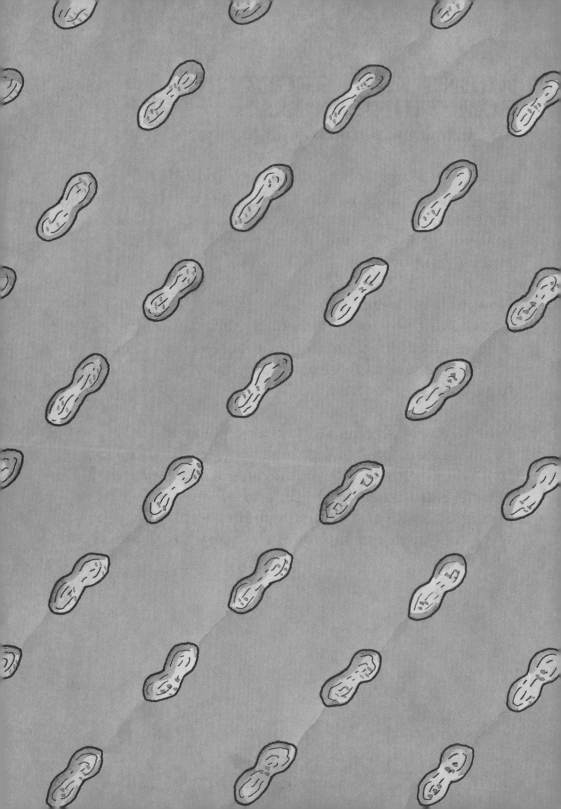

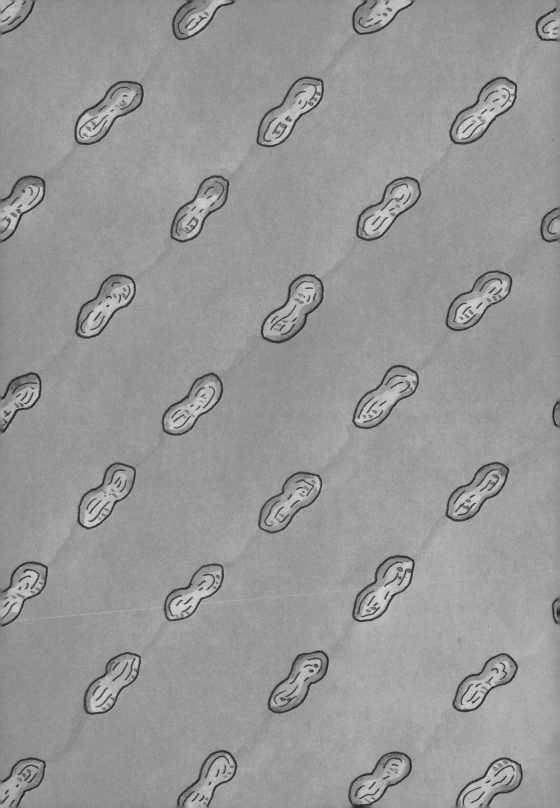

For a free color catalog describing Gareth Stevens' list of high-quality books, call 1-800-341-3569 (USA) or 1-800-461-9120 (Canada).

Parents Magazine READ ALOUD Originals:

Golly Gump Swallowed a Fly
The Housekeeper's Dog
Who Put the Pepper in the Pot?
Those Terrible Toy-Breakers
The Ghost in Dobbs Diner
The Biggest Shadow in the Zoo
The Old Man and the Afternoon Cat
Septimus Bean and His Amazing Machine
Sherlock Chick's First Case
A Garden for Miss Mouse
Witches Four
Bread and Honey
Pigs in the House
Milk and Cookies
But No Elephants
No Carrots for Harry!
Snow Lion
Henry's Awful Mistake
The Fox with Cold Feet
Get Well, Clown-Arounds!
Pets I Wouldn't Pick
Sherlock Chick and the Giant
   Egg Mystery
Cats! Cats! Cats!

Henry's Important Date
Elephant Goes to School
Rabbit's New Rug
Sand Cake
Socks for Supper
The Clown-Arounds Go on Vacation
The Little Witch Sisters
The Very Bumpy Bus Ride
Henry Babysits
There's No Place Like Home
Up Goes Mr. Downs
Bicycle Bear
Sweet Dreams, Clown-Arounds!
The Man Who Cooked for Himself
Where's Rufus?
The Giggle Book
Pickle Things
Oh, So Silly!
The Peace-and-Quiet Diner
Ten Furry Monsters
One Little Monkey
The Silly Tail Book
Aren't You Forgetting Something, Fiona?

Library of Congress Cataloging-in-Publication Data

Cole, Joanna.
   Aren't you forgetting something, Fiona? / by Joanna Cole; pictures by Ned Delaney.
      p. cm. — (Parents magazine read aloud original)
   "North American library edition"—T.p. verso.
   Summary: With the help of her family, Fiona, who has trouble remembering even the simplest, everyday things, remembers to go to exercise class with her best friend.
   ISBN 0-8368-0981-5
   [1. Memory—Fiction. 2. Elephants—Fiction.] I. Delaney, Ned, ill. II. Title. III. Series.
PZ7.C67346Ar 1994
[E]—dc20
                                                  93-36110

This North American library edition published in 1994 by Gareth Stevens Publishing, 1555 North RiverCenter Drive, Suite 201, Milwaukee, Wisconsin 53212, USA, under an arrangement with Parents Magazine Press, New York.

Printed in the United States of America

1 2 3 4 5 6 7 8 9 99 98 97 96 95 94

Aren't You Forgetting Something, Fiona?

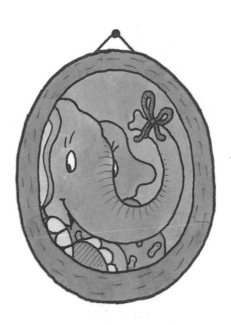

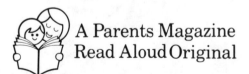

A Parents Magazine
Read Aloud Original

Aren't You Forgetting Something, Fiona?

by Joanna Cole
pictures by Ned Delaney

Gareth Stevens Publishing
Milwaukee
Parents Magazine Press
New York

To Shaina Feinberg—J.C.

To Bob Longley—N.D.

Aren't You Forgetting Something, Fiona?

In Fiona's family everyone was
good at remembering things.
Everyone except Fiona.

Fiona's mother always remembered
where she put things.

I knew it was here.

Fiona's father remembered all his
Aunt Sophie's best recipes.

Fiona's grandmother remembered
the words to every song she ever heard.

And Fiona's brother, Tim, remembered
every bad thing Fiona had ever done to him.

But Fiona had trouble remembering
even the simplest things.

If her mother asked her to get one thing,

she came back with something else.

Aren't you forgetting something, Fiona?

Even when she went out to play, Fiona was forgetful.

One day Fiona signed up for
an exercise class with
her best friend, Felicity.

But the day before class,
Fiona began to worry.

What if she forgot her gym clothes?
What if she forgot to go to class at all?
Fiona decided to ask her family for help.

"Make a big X on the calendar to remind yourself which day it is," said Tim.

"Put a note up telling yourself to go to class," said Grandmother. "Leave your gym bag by the door," said Father.

"And tie a ribbon around your trunk,"
said Mother. "Every time you see the
ribbon, it will remind you that there
is something special to remember."

Fiona did it all.

The next morning she saw the X,
read the note, picked up her bag,
and left the house right after breakfast.

But it was too good to last.
Fiona forgot where she was going.
She went up one street and down another.

30

Then she noticed the ribbon on her trunk.
"If I am wearing a ribbon, I must be
going to a party," thought Fiona.
"Maybe it is Felicity's birthday."

Fiona ran to the store for a present.
Then she set out for Felicity's house.

She hadn't gone far when she saw
Felicity poke her head out a window.
Then Fiona remembered her gym class.

Fiona gave Felicity the present anyway.
"My birthday isn't until next month,"
said Felicity. "But thank you, Fiona."

The present made jumping exercises
a lot more fun. And Fiona's ribbon
made a great headband.

Knee bend

That night, Fiona showed her family
what she'd learned in class.
She remembered everything.

Handstand

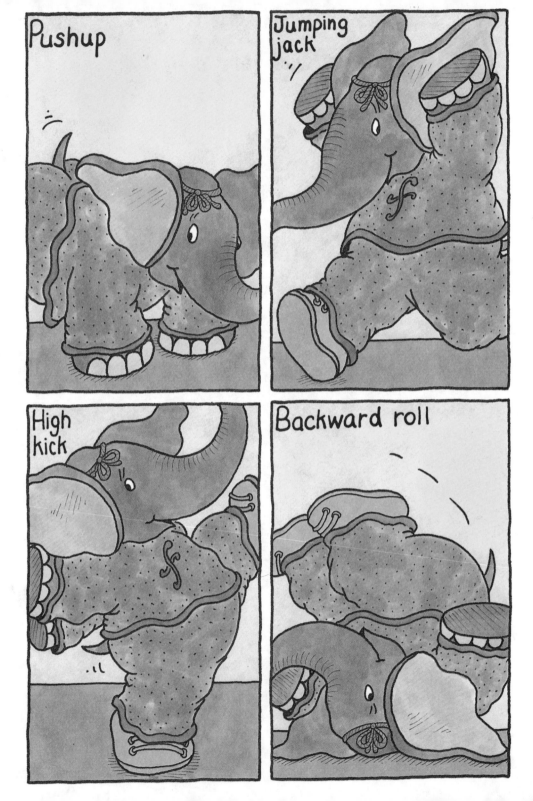

Her family was very proud of her.

Peanuts

And Fiona was proud of herself.

She went off happily to take her bath
and get ready for bed.
It had been a fine day—
one Fiona would remember for a long time!

Notes to Grown-ups

Major Themes

Here is a quick guide to the significant themes and concepts at work in *Aren't You Forgetting Something, Fiona?*:

- Family support: Fiona's family continually helped her and gave her hints in remembering.
- Memory: We can get into trouble when we forget to do important things, as Fiona knew so well.

Step-by-step Ideas for Reading and Talking

Here are some ideas for further give-and-take between grown-ups and children. The following topics encourage creative discussion of *Aren't You Forgetting Something, Fiona?* and invite the kind of open-ended response that is consistent with many contemporary approaches to reading, including Whole Language:

- Did the clues Fiona used to remember her class really work? Can you think of any other ways to remember important things?
- Are there any things we should try to forget? What about Tim's list of bad things Fiona had done? Would it be better if he forgot them? Even people who can forgive sometimes find it hard to forget.
- Fiona remembered the exercises she had learned in gym class. She forgot *objects* but she remembered *actions*. It might help an object-forgetter to prepare ahead of time for certain occasions. For example, the night before a picnic, skating party, or camping trip, gather most or all of the supplies or equipment you will need and place it near the door of your room or house entrance. This type of related activity will help you remember what you have planned.

Games for Learning

Games and activities can stimulate young readers and listeners alike to find out more about words, numbers, and ideas. Here are more ideas for turning learning into fun:

Junk Basket Relay

Memory skills are something we are born with, and yet, with practice and memory techniques, we can always improve. In a young child's development, the ability to follow one-step, and then two-step and three-step directions improves with practice and maturity. Here's a fun game to help your child practice and improve the ability to remember things in sequence.

To set up:
Collect a variety of unbreakable objects and set them in a laundry basket at one end of a room or backyard. At the other end of the space you have chosen, set an empty laundry basket.

To prepare your child:
Tell your child you are going to have him or her get several things, do something with them, and run back to you. Show your child an example, walking through one of the suggested directions below:

Go get a __ and a __ and hop them over to the empty basket.

Variations: crawl, skip, twirl, jump, run, wiggle

About the Author

Once, before going on vacation, JOANNA COLE hid some jewelry in a safe place. When she came back, she forgot where she had hidden it. A year later, while cleaning out a cupboard, she was happily surprised to find it. "I like to think that, like Fiona, I remember the important things," she says.

About the Artist

NED DELANEY has been writing and illustrating picture books since he graduated from college. He teaches writing and illustrating at Salem State College in Massachusetts.

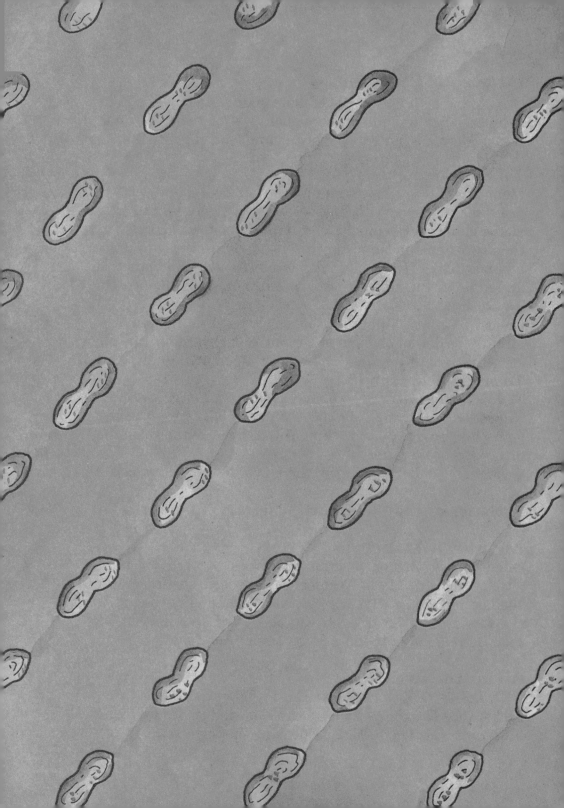

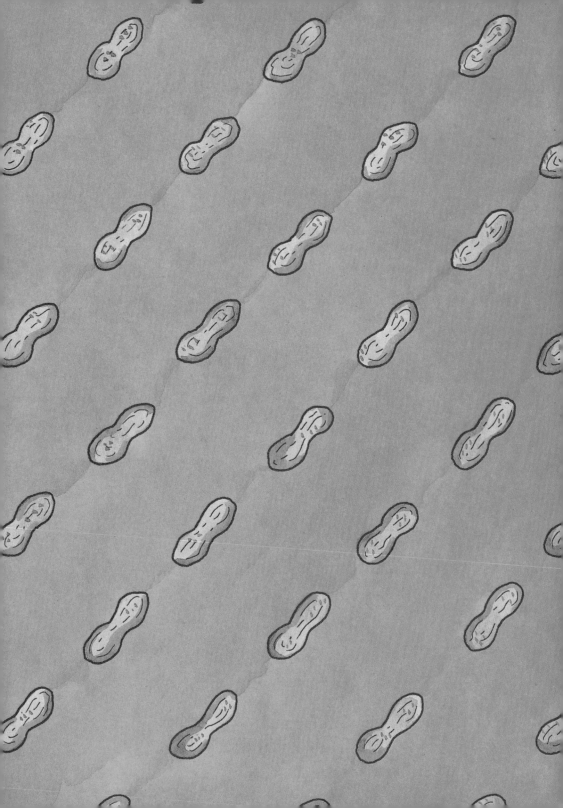